SOMEONE
for
MR. SUSSMAN

For all of those who are crooked pots
who have finally found a lid.

Patricia Polacco
SOMEONE
for
MR. SUSSMAN

PHILOMEL BOOKS

My bubbie is a *shadkhen*. If you're not Jewish, you may not know what a *shadkhen* is. You see, people come to my bubbie—my grandmother—to help them find a wife or a husband. She finds her clients the perfect match!

My bubbie is a very successful matchmaker. She has dozens of very happy clients. Finding a person the perfect match is so easy for her.

Except for one man: Mr. Sussman!

I mean, she found a widow for Mr. Bushbaum down the hall, and that wasn't easy.

A podiatrist for the Turtletaubs' daughter, and that was impossible.

Even a wife for the Firesteins' very large son, and that was a miracle!

She found the perfect match for everyone . . . except Mr. Sussman.

He seemed to be her favorite client, though. She always looked forward to his coming over. I never really understood why.

"Come in, Mr. Sussman . . . sit . . . sit," she'd say.

"Oy, my feet. I walked all the way from Tenth Avenue," he'd say as he made for the best chair in the apartment.

"*Your* feet! Mine should walk another inch without falling off," Bubbie would exclaim.

"We are so alike, Mrs. Zukin," Mr. Sussman said.

"Alike!" she agreed as she smiled.

One day, shortly after Mr. Sussman arrived, he furrowed his brow.

"Matchmaker, I've been thinking about a perfect match. I think I know exactly what I am looking for at long last," Mr. Sussman said as he looked at the ceiling thoughtfully.

My bubbie jotted notes on her pad and leaned forward.

"I would like to find someone who remembers the old country . . . a woman who keeps a kosher house, maybe. Someone very observant!" Mr. Sussman said.

What does *kosher* mean, you ask. The food observant Jews eat has to be
prepared in a very special way. They can never mix meat and dairy on the
same plate, so they usually have two sets of dishes. They can't even touch
meat and dairy with the same fork or spoon or knife. If that happens, the
flatware has to be put in a flowerpot full of dirt for a long time.

My bubbie thought for a moment after hearing Mr. Sussman's request
and then answered. "This person I'll find for you. It'll be the perfect
match!" she assured him, and sent him on his way.

After he left that day, I said, "Bubbie, that one you'll never please. You'll never find him a perfect match. He's so picky!"

"No pot is so crooked that there isn't a lid to fit it!" Bubbie sang out.

Before Mr. Sussman arrived for his next appointment, Bubbie sent me on many errands.

"Please, Jerome, go over to Mrs. Robinski's and borrow her Pishky box, some of her clothes . . . a full set of her dishes. We have to have different sets for dairy and meat!"

I did as she asked.

When Mr. Sussman arrived, Bubbie was ready for him.
"Shalom!" she greeted him.

"Mrs. Zukin," he replied. "Never have I seen you in this light before. So serene. So observant!" he said with reverence. "Never have I noticed that you have so . . . many dishes!"

"My late husband Bernard was very observant, as am I, Mr. Sussman. This is a kosher house. I have dishes for dairy and dishes for meat . . . and look, my silver garden," my bubbie said as she adjusted the flowerpot.

"Too many dishes. I can't even see out of your kitchen window!" Mr. Sussman said sternly.

He sat back in his favorite chair.

"Matchmaker, I've been thinking," Mr. Sussman began. "I would like you to find me someone who loves color . . . lots of color. Blue! That's it. Blue is my favorite color."

"This person I'll find for you!" my bubbie assured him, and sent him on his way.

"Too picky," I whispered to Bubbie as he left.

For the next few days, my bubbie took me to every fabric store in the garment district. She bought bolts and bolts of blue. She bought every piece of cloth she could find that was blue. Print, floral, stripes and checks.

When Mr. Sussman arrived for his next appointment, Bubbie was ready for him.

"Mrs. Zukin!" he exclaimed. "The apartment . . . have you done something new to it?"

"Why, yes!" my bubbie cooed.

"Nice . . . but too much blue!" Mr. Sussman said sternly.

He then took his usual seat in the easy chair.
"Matchmaker, I've been thinking," he began. "I would like you to find
me someone who is a wonderful cook. No. Someone who bakes!"

My bubbie took notes in her pad.

"This I'll find for you!" she assured him, and sent him on his way.

"Picky, picky, picky," I whispered to Bubbie, a little louder this time.

On the morning of Mr. Sussman's next appointment, my bubbie sent me on a spree, buying every baked good that I could find from all of the kosher bakeshops and delis.

"Jerome, the best, get the best!" she called out as I left.

I went. I got bagels, kugel, blintzes, finger cake, challah, cookies, buns, rolls, and even matzoh.

When Mr. Sussman arrived, Bubbie was ready for him.

"Come in, Mr. Sussman. You'll have to excuse me, but I have been doing a little baking," Bubbie said.

"A little!" Mr. Sussman exclaimed as he eyed the dazzling display of baked goods.

"Baking like this I have never seen!" he snorted, jumping up as he sat right on a prune danish.

"I do it just to pass the time, Mr. Sussman," my bubbie babbled. "A kugel, a blintz, or perhaps a nice knish?"

"All this sweet bread. Doughy. This will make me sick . . . I'll have gas!" Mr. Sussman said sternly.

Then he took his seat by the window again.

"Matchmaker, I've been thinking," he began. "I would like you to find me someone who is very health-minded . . . fit . . . someone who doesn't overeat and who likes to walk, maybe," he said thoughtfully. "Takes long walks in the park."

Bubbie made notes in her pad. She sighed.

"This person, Mr. Sussman, I'll find for you!" my bubbie assured him, and sent him on his way.

After he left, she leaned over to me.

"I know, too picky. You don't have to say it," she whispered.

A day or two before Mr. Sussman's next appointment, Bubbie rented gym equipment and had it delivered. She got everything. Stair steppers, thigh busters, barbells, a treadmill and even a rowing machine.

When Mr. Sussman arrived, Bubbie was ready for him.

"Mrs. Zukin!" Mr. Sussman said with surprise. "What are you wearing, already?"

"Sweats, Mr. Sussman," she answered energetically. "I'm so into health, you know. I do a little running . . . a little rowing . . . a little swimming . . . I lift, Mr. Sussman. Free weights!"

"Oy, you're making me tired just thinking on it, Mrs. Zukin!" he said as he oozed into the easy chair
by the window.

"Matchmaker, I've been thinking about my perfect match," Mr. Sussman said. "I want you to find me a woman who loves to dance! That's it. That's what I want."

Bubbie made notes, sighed, clenched her teeth, sighed again, took a deep breath and jotted more notes.

She looked at Mr. Sussman for a long time.

"This person I'll find for you," my bubbie hissed, and sent him on his way.

Bubbie was so farklempt, I didn't have the heart to say anything this time.

But for the whole next week Bubbie dragged me along to the Ali Baba Dance Palace. We went every single day. We learned the samba, the fox-trot, the waltz, boogie-woogie, bebop and salsa.

We practiced and practiced.

The next time Mr. Sussman arrived for his appointment, Bubbie was ready for him.

"Mrs. Zukin, what is that getup you have on?" Mr. Sussman asked in astonishment.

"Jerome, the music, please!" Bubbie cued me as I turned on the salsa.

Bubbie grabbed Mr. Sussman and bent him over her arm. She began to dance him all over the room.

"Enough . . . enough already!" Mr. Sussman collapsed into her easy chair in complete exhaustion.

"Matchmaker," he finally wheezed. "I've been thinking—"

"Thinking . . . thinking . . . that's all you do, Mr. Sussman. I don't think I will EVER be able to find a match for you. It's impossible! A matchmaker you don't need, Mr. Sussman. A MIRACLE you need!"

Bubbie snapped shut her appointment book.

"No more appointments, Mr. Sussman."

And she sent him on his way.

Then Bubbie just sat in the chair by the window and looked out.

My bubbie wouldn't see Mr. Sussman after that.

Then one day, the doorbell rang. It was Mr. Sussman. Bubbie was shocked to see him. So was I.

"I was just in the neighborhood, Mrs. Zukin."

"Come in, Mr. Sussman," Bubbie said quietly.

"I will, Mrs. Zukin. Thank you," he replied.

Bubbie offered him the easy chair. He sat down and looked around.

"Everything looks so different. I've never noticed how homey and warm your apartment is," he said as Bubbie served him a cup of lemon tea.

"This is my favorite tea, Mrs. Zukin. Why have you never offered me this before?" he asked as he sipped it.

Bubbie just smiled.

"It's so peaceful. No loud music. No piles of dishes everywhere, and all that awful blue fabric is gone," he said quietly.

Bubbie just smiled.

"Where's the treadmill that was in the hall?" he asked.

Bubbie didn't answer. She just listened. She leaned in to him with a plate of ginger cookies.

"You know, Mrs. Zukin, I've never really noticed what beautiful eyes you have," Mr. Sussman said as he peered into them. "What soft hands you have," he said as he took her hands into his.

"And here you've been. Right in front of me, all this time. You are such a person, Mrs. Zukin . . . such a person!" Mr. Sussman said softly.

"I thought you'd never notice," Bubbie said breathlessly.

"I'm noticing . . . I'm noticing," Mr. Sussman said dreamily.

Then Bubbie smiled such a smile that I knew Mr. Sussman had found what he had been looking for all along. I wasn't surprised.

Their wedding was the event of the neighborhood.

My bubbie and Mr. Sussman keep a kosher kitchen together now. After
all, they have two sets of dishes.

Bubbie learned to bake. Her knishes and blintzes are almost as good as
Fishbine's Deli. Mr. Sussman loves absolutely everything about my bubbie!

They are so happy together. A perfect match.

And, I thought to myself, Bubbie was right, you know . . .

"No pot is so crooked that there isn't a lid to fit it!"

PATRICIA LEE GAUCH, EDITOR

PHILOMEL BOOKS
A division of Penguin Young Readers Group.
Published by The Penguin Group.
Penguin Group (USA) Inc., 375 Hudson Street, New York, NY 10014, U.S.A.
Penguin Group (Canada), 90 Eglinton Avenue East, Suite 700, Toronto, Ontario M4P 2Y3, Canada (a division of Pearson Penguin Canada Inc.).
Penguin Books Ltd, 80 Strand, London WC2R 0RL, England.
Penguin Ireland, 25 St. Stephen's Green, Dublin 2, Ireland (a division of Penguin Books Ltd).
Penguin Group (Australia), 250 Camberwell Road, Camberwell, Victoria 3124, Australia (a division of Pearson Australia Group Pty Ltd).
Penguin Books India Pvt Ltd, 11 Community Centre, Panchsheel Park, New Delhi - 110 017, India.
Penguin Group (NZ), 67 Apollo Drive, Rosedale, North Shore 0632, New Zealand (a division of Pearson New Zealand Ltd).
Penguin Books (South Africa) (Pty) Ltd, 24 Sturdee Avenue, Rosebank, Johannesburg 2196, South Africa.
Penguin Books Ltd, Registered Offices: 80 Strand, London WC2R 0RL, England.

Copyright © 2008 by Babushka Inc.

Published simultaneously in Canada.   Manufactured in China by South China Printing Co. Ltd.
Design by Semadar Megged.   Text set in 15.5-point Adobe Jenson.   The illustrations are rendered in pencils and markers.
Library of Congress Cataloging-in-Publication Data is available upon request.
ISBN 978-0-399-25075-0
1 3 5 7 9 10 8 6 4 2